Tiger Eyes

Level 11 – Lime

Helpful Hints for Reading at Home

The focus phonemes (units of sound) used throughout this series are in line with the order in which your child is taught at school. This offers a consistent approach to learning whether reading at home or in the classroom.

HERE ARE SOME COMMON WORDS THAT YOUR CHILD MIGHT FIND TRICKY:

water	where	would	know	thought	through	couldn't
laughed	eyes	once	we're	school	can't	our

TOP TIPS FOR HELPING YOUR CHILD TO READ:

- Encourage your child to read aloud as well as silently to themselves.
- Allow your child time to absorb the text and make comments.
- Ask simple questions about the text to assess understanding.
- Encourage your child to clarify the meaning of new vocabulary.

This book focuses on developing independence, fluency and comprehension. It is a lime level 11 book band.

Tiger Eyes

Written by
Kirsty Holmes

Illustrated by
Drue Rintoul

Chapter One

In the Jungle

It was a hot, sticky morning, deep in the jungle. Madison Green had been up and about for quite a while. Madison liked to take pictures with her camera early in the morning. She liked the way the light shone through the trees and left a dappled pattern on the ground. On this morning, she was taking pictures of some very cool caterpillars she had found.

You might be wondering why Madison was taking pictures of caterpillars instead of getting ready for school. She was twelve years old, after all. Madison, you see, came from a family that wasn't like most families, and Madison didn't live in a place where you can easily get to school. At the start of our story, Madison lived in the middle of the jungle!

Madison's mum was a famous botanist. A botanist is a kind of scientist who knows all about plants. She was looking for some rare and special flowers in this part of the jungle. Madison's dad was the star of a popular television show all about animals. His favourite animals were tigers. Madison had a channel on social media. Here, she showed other children what life was like for the girl who lived in the jungle.

Madison's channel was very popular. She made videos showing people how she and her family were working to look after the planet. These projects were very important to Madison and she liked to show other people. She called them Madison's Missions. The Green family were on a mission to save nature, and Madison made sure she let the whole world know.

"Hi guys! Welcome back to Madison's Missions! So, did you figure it out? That's right! We

vEejit

have just arrived in the jungle! We're here for a really, really special reason. The amazing trees you see behind me were going to be cut down, but we think we might have found a reason to save them. The Green family are on a mission to find... Tigers!"

If Madison and her family could find proof that there were tigers living in this part of the jungle, then it would be a nature park. Madison was really excited to be part of something so special. She had packed all her special cameras in the hope of maybe, just maybe, getting to take a picture of a tiger herself!

On the first morning, they set up the camp.
Madison was unpacking her bag and settling
in. She noticed a small, green lizard looking
up at her from the floor next to her bunk.
"Hello there!" she said. "What are you doing
down there?"
The lizard looked at her. It flicked its pink
tongue in and out and caught a passing fly.

Madison tried to unpack but the little lizard
did not seem to want to leave her alone!
In the end, she put him on her shoulder and
he seemed quite happy up there.
She got on with helping to
set up the camp. She
was excited to go out
and look around.
Would they see
a tiger today?
She picked up
her camera
excitedly.

"If you're going to stick around, little guy," she said, "you're going to need a name." Madison looked at the small lizard now sitting happily in her hand. It had bumpy green skin, and long, scaly toes. Its tail was long and curly, too. It had round, rolling eyes like glass marbles. Madison thought he was kind of cute.

"I think I will call you Herbert," said Madison. "You look like a Herbert." Herbert rolled his eyes again. Madison decided that meant he liked his new name. She put him down on the bed and took her camera from her bag. Click. Click. Click. Herbert seemed to like having his picture taken. Madison giggled. She liked her new little friend.

In the late afternoon, Madison and her parents went into the jungle to look for proof of tigers.

"Will we see a tiger today, Dad?" asked Madison.

"Maybe," said Dad. "Maybe not. Tigers are very good at hiding."

"That's why we have got to look for other proof," said Mum.

Suddenly, Dad stopped.

"Look!" he said. "Tracks!"

"Is it a tiger, Dad?" asked Madison.

"Hmm. It's a bit smudged," said Dad.

"I'll try and take a plaster cast," said Mum. "Why don't you two go on ahead? I'll catch up."

Mum got out a little mixing bowl and some plaster and water to make a mould of the paw print. Madison and Dad moved on.

Madison and her dad walked into the jungle.
"Will Mum be OK, Dad?" asked Madison.
"Oh yes," said Dad. "She's been doing this
for a long time. You have to learn to be still
and quiet when you work in nature. You also
get used to being alone. Once, I waited
almost nineteen hours to take a photo of
a very rare cat."

"That's ages, Dad!" said Madison. "Did you
take a good picture?"
"No," Dad laughed. "I waited nineteen hours
and I missed it."
"What happened?" Madison's eyes were wide.
"I went behind the tree for a wee. When I
came back, I just saw its tail as it ran away."
Madison giggled.
"Oh, Dad," she said.

Just then, Madison stepped in something soft and sticky. Squelch!

"Oh Dad! I stepped in something!" she said. Madison looked down. Oh, no. She had stepped in a huge poo!

"Don't move!" said Dad. "That might be tiger poo!"

Madison had never been so happy about accidentally stepping in poo! Could this be the proof?

Dad scraped a sample of the poo from Madison's boot. He put it in a little pot and put the pot in his pocket. Madison got her camera and took some photos of the poo. They looked around a little for more clues. After a while, Dad looked at his watch.

"Time to head back to camp," he said.

Chapter Two

Tiger Eyes

"Hi guys! Welcome back to Madison's Missions! We've been in the jungle for a few weeks now. We have got part of a paw print that might belong to a tiger, but we aren't sure. We found some poo, and after that, nothing. Mum and I set up some camera traps. They only come on if anything walks past. We're going to check them today."

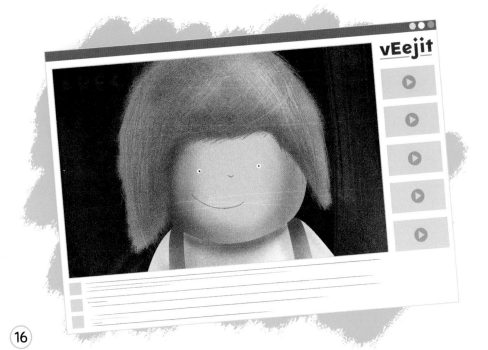

Madison and her mum were checking the camera traps. To get to the traps, they followed a map that Mum had drawn. The map showed where all the traps were so they would not forget. When they got there, Madison carefully took out the card with the videos on. They put a new battery in and set the traps again.

"Fingers crossed," said Mum.

Back at camp, Madison found Herbert sitting in her bed.

"Oh, Herbert. I really hope there is something to see on this video," she said.

Herbert looked up at her and did a little dance. He wiggled his tail and bobbed his head. Madison decided this was a good luck dance. She danced too.

Mum put the videos from the camera traps in the computer. The film from the traps was grey and fuzzy. First, two small birds with big fan tails went past, then flew away. Next, a huge animal that looked like a very big mouse ran by. There were many interesting animals to see on the video. But there were no tigers.

Everyone was a bit fed up. Mum and Dad looked like they were going to have a fight. Madison didn't like it when that happened. She got her camera and popped Herbert into her pocket.

"I think I will go and take some pictures of flowers," she said to herself.

The Sun was just going down, and the sky was a beautiful pink colour. Madison thought it made the jungle look very beautiful, and she walked to the edge of camp. Madison was not allowed to go into the jungle alone, so she found a good spot near the back of the camp and started to take her pictures.
Click.
Click.
Click.

Madison looked up and saw some bright orange flowers. Dad had said they were called tiger eyes. She used her camera to zoom in on the beautiful blooms. The flowers were bright orange. They were fluffy in the centre and had beautiful black stems. She had never seen anything like them before!

Suddenly, Madison dropped her camera and froze. Something was moving in the bushes. Dad had said that the jungle was a beautiful place, but there were animals who might think Madison looked like a tasty snack. Madison didn't want to be someone's dinner. She stood very still and didn't breathe.

Slowly, the flowers swayed and moved. Something was behind the flowers, Madison was sure. But what was it? She couldn't see anything. Maybe it was something small? A wild pig had run through the camp a few nights ago. It had been funny at the time. Perhaps it had come back?

Madison's hand was shaking. One of the flowers swayed gently, as if a breeze was blowing. But all of the other flowers were still. Was it a flower after all? It was bright orange. It had a fluffy black centre. Oh no. Madison thought to herself. Was that black and orange thing a flower? Or was it a tail?

The light from the setting Sun caught something shiny. It looked like two bright copper pennies, lit by the sunlight. Madison stared. Those shining things were a pair of eyes. Madison felt her heart jump. She couldn't breathe. She had seen those eyes in hundreds of pictures. She couldn't believe that she was looking at a tiger!

Madison was frozen to the spot. She watched as the huge cat moved in the grass like a shadow. She held her breath. The tiger walked along the path. His huge paws went pad, pad, pad. Madison's heart went thud, thud, thud. She could not move at all. Suddenly, there was a noise from camp. The tiger ran away.

Madison grabbed her
camera but it was
too late. The tiger
had gone, and
she hadn't got the
proof! Madison
walked sadly back
to camp. She wanted
to tell her parents that
she had seen the tiger. But what if that had
been their only chance to prove they were
there?

"Did I miss it?" thought Madison.

Back at camp, Madison was in a huff. She
threw her camera onto the floor by her tent.
Herbert ran over to it and rolled his eyes
at it. Then he climbed on top and went to
sleep. Madison was not in the mood for taking
pictures tonight anyway. She went into the
tent and lay on her bed. It was getting dark,
and Madison soon went to sleep too.

Chapter Three

The Last Morning

"Hi guys. Welcome back to Madison's Missions. Today, I have got sad news, guys. It's the last day of our trip to the jungle. We found some cool stuff, but we didn't get a picture of a tiger. Mum says we have to talk to the people who own the land and see if we can get more time. I just wish I'd been able to get one picture."

Mum and Dad had started to pack the camp away, ready to go home. There was no more time to find the tigers. Mum was very sad. Dad kept stopping to give her a hug. The packing was not going very well. Madison was packing her own things into her bag. She picked up her camera from the ground. Had it been on all night?

"Madison seems sad this morning," said Mum.
"I know," said Dad. "She was quiet last night, too."
"None of us want to go home. I just wish we had found the proof!" said Mum.
"Me too," sighed Dad. "Maybe the poo sample will be enough. I just wish we could have got one picture. Or even a video."

Madison looked at the camera. Herbert must have switched it on when he climbed up for his nap. She pressed the play button. She saw her mum's feet heading for their tent. Then, after a minute, her dad's feet heading for the food tent. She pressed fast forward.

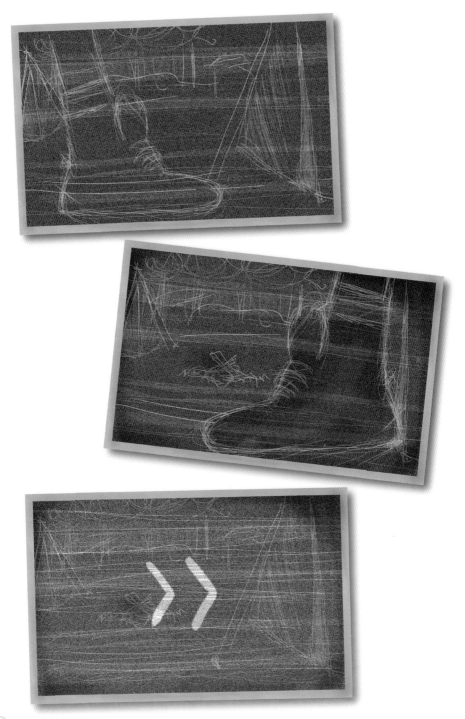

Madison froze. She played the video back.
She was so surprised by what she saw that
she almost dropped the camera again. There
was a tiger on the video! A real, actual tiger!
It must have been the big one that she saw by
the flowers. There it was, walking right across
camp!

"Mum! Dad! You have to see this!" shouted
Madison.

When the tiger walked across the screen, Mum
started to cry. Herbert did his little dance
and Dad and Madison did too. They were all
so happy that they almost didn't notice the
second tiger cross the screen. It was a good
thing Mum spotted it. Following the second
tiger was a baby tiger cub!

Dad got on the radio at once.
"A family!" he said over and over again.
"A real tiger family!"
Mum kept running over to Madison and
hugging her.
"We did it!" Mum said, over and over again.
"We did it!"

Chapter Four

What Happened Next

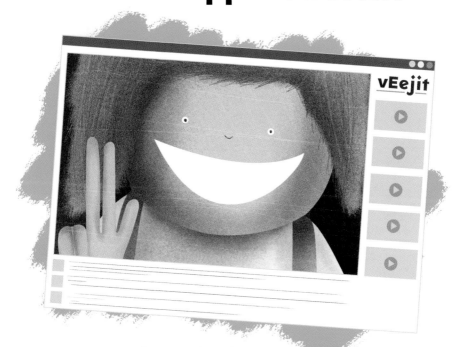

"Hi guys! Welcome back to Madison's Missions! This is a mission update for you all. So, you all know we found not one, not two, but three tigers out here in the jungle. Well, that's just the beginning! We showed our video to the people who own this land. They knew they just had to save this little family of big cats."

The jungle was saved! Madison felt happy and proud. The people who owned the land decided to make it a special park. The tigers were safe and so were all the other animals who lived there. Madison and her family went to the grand opening. Madison wore her favourite outfit.

Madison's videos about the tiger search were very popular. They were on every internet site and even on the TV! Madison was suddenly very famous. She told everyone about her family, and the story of how Madison's video saved a forest was talked about all over the world. Madison even got to go on the news!

"But the best bit of all was this. I got this very special letter today. It is from a place called the UN. All

the people at the UN work hard to protect the world. It's like a big, important club. They have asked me to go and speak to them about the tigers. Everyone in the world will be listening. I'm so excited!"

Madison stood up in front of all the grown-ups at the United Nations and told them all about the tigers. She told them about the other creatures they had seen in the jungle. She asked them all to work hard to protect the tigers. Madison was so happy. The people at the UN agreed to protect the tigers and the jungle too. Mission success!

"So that's the end of this story! The tigers are now protected and the jungle is safe. I love being the girl who lives in the jungle, but it is also nice to be home. Mum and Dad and I are going to have a rest. But don't worry! Madison's Missions will be back soon. There is always a new adventure to go on! Mission success!"

But that wasn't even the best bit. Mum and Dad were so proud of Madison that they got her a very special present. It was a tiny, fluffy kitten! The kitten was orange and black and stripy.
"What will you name him, Madison?" asked Mum.
"I think I will name him Tiger," said Madison.

Tiger Eyes

1.   How old is Madison?

2.   What did Madison decide was Herbert's good luck dance?

3.   What did Dad say were called tiger eyes?
     (a)   Green flowers
     (b)   Fireflies
     (c)   Orange flowers

4.   Why do you think Mum started to cry when she saw the tiger on the screen?

5.   Why do you think the United Nations invited Madison to speak about the tigers? Do you think this is important?

©2020 **BookLife Publishing Ltd.**
King's Lynn, Norfolk PE30 4LS

ISBN 978-1-83927-022-2

A catalogue record for this book is available from the British Library.

Tiger Eyes
Written by Kirsty Holmes
Illustrated by Drue Rintoul

An Introduction to BookLife Readers...

Our Readers have been specifically created in line with the London Institute of Education's approach to book banding and are phonetically decodable and ordered to support each phase of the Letters and Sounds document.

Each book has been created to provide the best possible reading and learning experience. Our aim is to share our love of books with children, providing both emerging readers and prolific page-turners with beautiful books that are guaranteed to provoke interest and learning, regardless of ability.

BOOK BAND GRADED using the Institute of Education's approach to levelling.

PHONETICALLY DECODABLE supporting each phase of Letters and Sounds.

EXERCISES AND QUESTIONS to offer reinforcement and to ascertain comprehension.

BEAUTIFULLY ILLUSTRATED to inspire and provoke engagement, providing a variety of styles for the reader to enjoy whilst reading through the series.

AUTHOR INSIGHT: KIRSTY HOLMES

Kirsty Holmes, holder of a BA, PGCE, and an MA, was born in Norfolk, England. She has written over 60 books for BookLife Publishing, and her stories are full of imagination, creativity and fun.

This book focuses on developing independence, fluency and comprehension. It is a lime level 11 book band.